An I Can Read Book®

The Amelia Bedelia TREASURY

Three Books by Peggy Parish

Illustrated by Fritz Siebel and
Barbara Siebel Thomas

HarperCollinsPublishers

For Debbie, John Grier,

Walter, and Michael Dinkins

ISBN: 0-06-026787-9

CONTENTS

An I Can Read Book®

Amelia Bedelia

by Peggy Parish

Pictures by Fritz Siebel

"Oh, Amelia Bedelia,

your first day of work,

and I can't be here.

But I made a list for you.

You do just what the list says,"

said Mrs. Rogers.

Mrs. Rogers got into the car

with Mr. Rogers.

They drove away.

"My, what nice folks.
I'm going to like working here,"
said Amelia Bedelia.

And please dress the chicken.

Amelia Bedelia went inside.
"Such a grand house.
These must be rich folks.
But I must get to work.
Here I stand just looking.
And me with a whole list
of things to do."
Amelia Bedelia stood there
a minute longer.
"I think I'll make
a surprise for them.
I'll make lemon-meringue pie.
I do make good pies."

So Amelia Bedelia went
into the kitchen.
She put a little of this
and a pinch of that
into a bowl.
She mixed and she rolled.

Soon her pie was ready
to go into the oven.
"There," said Amelia Bedelia.
"That's done.

"Now let's see what this list says."

Amelia Bedelia read,

Change the towels in the green bathroom.

Amelia Bedelia found
the green bathroom.
"Those towels are very nice.
Why change them?" she thought.

Then Amelia Bedelia remembered
what Mrs. Rogers had said.
She must do just what
the list told her.
"Well, all right,"
said Amelia Bedelia.
Amelia Bedelia got some scissors.
She snipped a little here
and a little there.
And she changed those towels.

"There," said Amelia Bedelia.

She looked at her list again.

Dust the furniture.

"Did you ever hear tell

of such a silly thing.

At my house we undust the furniture.

But to each his own way."

Amelia Bedelia took
one last look at the bathroom.
She saw a big box with the words
Dusting Powder on it.

"Well, look at that.
A special powder to dust with!"
exclaimed Amelia Bedelia.
So Amelia Bedelia
dusted the furniture.
"That should be dusty enough.
My, how nice it smells."

Draw the drapes when the sun comes in.

read Amelia Bedelia.

She looked up.

The sun was coming in.

Amelia Bedelia looked

at the list again.

"Draw the drapes?

That's what it says.

I'm not much

of a hand at drawing,

but I'll try."

So Amelia Bedelia sat right down
and she drew those drapes.

Amelia Bedelia

marked off

about the drapes.

"Now what?"

Put the lights out when you finish in the living room.

Amelia Bedelia

thought about this a minute.

She switched off the lights.

Then she carefully

unscrewed each bulb.

And Amelia Bedelia
put the lights out.
"So those things need
to be aired out, too.
Just like pillows and babies.
Oh, I do have a lot to learn."

"My pie!" exclaimed Amelia Bedelia.

She hurried to the kitchen.

“Just right,” she said.

She took the pie out of the oven

and put it on the table to cool.

Then she looked at the list.

Measure two cups of rice.

"That's next," said Amelia Bedelia.

Amelia Bedelia found two cups.

She filled them with rice.

And Amelia Bedelia
measured that rice.

Amelia Bedelia laughed.

"These folks

do want me to do funny things."

Then she poured the rice

back into the container.

The meat market will deliver a steak and a chicken.

Please trim the fat before you put the steak in the icebox.

And please dress the chicken.

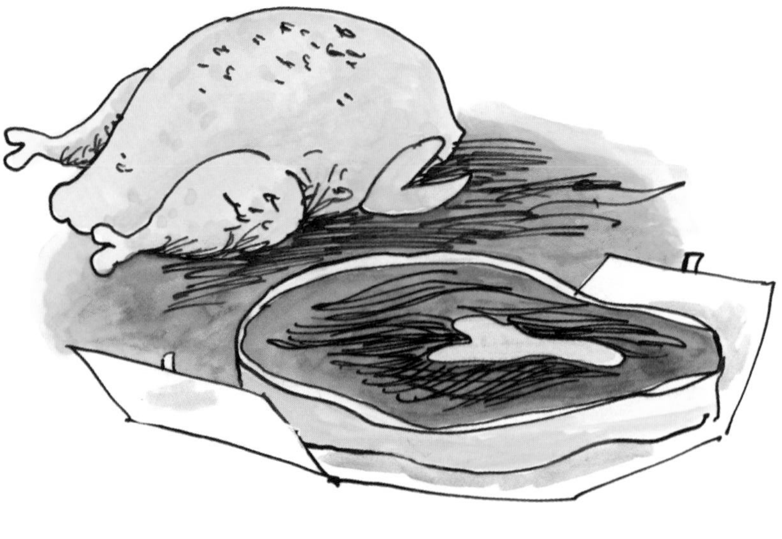

When the meat arrived,

Amelia Bedelia opened the bag.

She looked at the steak

for a long time.

"Yes," she said.

"That will do nicely."

Amelia Bedelia got some lace
and bits of ribbon.
And Amelia Bedelia
trimmed that fat
before she put
the steak in the icebox.

"Now I must dress the chicken.

I wonder if she wants

a he chicken or a she chicken?"

said Amelia Bedelia.

Amelia Bedelia went right to work.

Soon the chicken was finished.

Amelia Bedelia heard the door open.

"The folks are back," she said.

She rushed out to meet them.

"Amelia Bedelia,
why are all the light bulbs outside?"
asked Mr. Rogers.

"The list just said
to put the lights out,"
said Amelia Bedelia.
"It didn't say to bring them back in.
Oh, I do hope
they didn't get aired too long."

"Amelia Bedelia,

the sun will fade the furniture.

I asked you to draw the drapes,"

said Mrs. Rogers.

"I did! I did! See,"

said Amelia Bedelia.

She held up her picture.

Then Mrs. Rogers saw the furniture.

"The furniture!" she cried.

"Did I dust it well enough?"

asked Amelia Bedelia.

"That's such nice dusting powder."

Mr. Rogers went to wash his hands.

"I say," he called.

"These are very unusual towels."

Mrs. Rogers dashed into the bathroom.

"Oh, my best towels," she said.

"Didn't I change them enough?"

asked Amelia Bedelia.

Mrs. Rogers went to the kitchen.

"I'll cook the dinner.

Where is the rice

I asked you to measure?"

“I put it back in the container.
But I remember–
it measured four and a half inches,”
said Amelia Bedelia.

"Was the meat delivered?"
asked Mrs. Rogers.
"Yes," said Amelia Bedelia.
"I trimmed the fat just like you said.
It does look nice."
Mrs. Rogers rushed to the icebox.
She opened it.
"Lace! Ribbons!
Oh, dear!" said Mrs. Rogers.

MILK
FISH

"The chicken—you dressed
the chicken?"
asked Mrs. Rogers.
"Yes, and I found the nicest box
to put him in,"
said Amelia Bedelia.
"Box!" exclaimed Mrs. Rogers.
Mrs. Rogers hurried over to the box.
She lifted the lid.
There lay the chicken.
And he was just as dressed
as he could be.

Mrs. Rogers was angry.

She was very angry.

She opened her mouth.

Mrs. Rogers meant

to tell Amelia Bedelia

she was fired.

But before she could

get the words out,

Mr. Rogers put something

in her mouth.

It was so good

Mrs. Rogers forgot about being angry.

"Lemon-meringue pie!"
she exclaimed.
"I made it to surprise you,"
said Amelia Bedelia happily.
So right then and there
Mr. and Mrs. Rogers decided
that Amelia Bedelia must stay.
And so she did.
Mrs. Rogers learned to say
undust the furniture,
unlight the lights,
close the drapes,
and things like that.

Mr. Rogers didn't care
if Amelia Bedelia
trimmed all
of his steaks with lace.

All he cared about
was having her there
to make lemon-meringue pie.

Thank You, Amelia Bedelia

An I Can Read Book®

Thank You, Amelia Bedelia

Story by Peggy Parish

Pictures by Barbara Siebel Thomas

based on the original drawings by Fritz Siebel

For Ann, Jack, and Brad Rost

Mrs. Rogers was all in a dither.

"Great-Aunt Myra

is coming today."

"Now, that is nice,"

said Amelia Bedelia.

"I do love company."

“We’ve been trying for years
to get her to visit,”
said Mrs. Rogers,
“but Great-Aunt Myra says
the only place she feels at home
is at home.
So everything must be exactly right.
We do want her to be happy here.”
“Now don’t you worry your head,”
said Amelia Bedelia.
“I’ll fix everything.
What should I do first?”

"Well, the guest room
must be made ready.
Strip the sheets off the bed.
Remake it
with the new rosebud sheets,"
said Mrs. Rogers.
"Thank goodness you're here."

Amelia Bedelia went

to the guest room.

"These folks do have odd ways.

Imagine stripping sheets

after you use them."

Amelia Bedelia shook her head.

But she stripped those sheets.

Amelia Bedelia had just finished
when the doorbell rang.
"That must be the laundryman
with Mr. Rogers's shirts,"
called Mrs. Rogers.
"Please check them
and make sure
they're all there."
Amelia Bedelia hurried to the door
and took the package.

Amelia Bedelia opened the package.

She unfolded each shirt.

“Two sleeves, one collar,

one pocket, and six buttons.

Yes, they’re all here.”

"There's not a thing missing,"
said Amelia Bedelia.
"Now to check them.
It would be a sight easier
to buy them already checked,"
said Amelia Bedelia.
But she quickly checked each shirt.

Mrs. Rogers

came downstairs in a rush.

"Amelia Bedelia,

my bright pink dress

has spots in it.

Please remove them

with this spot remover.

Leave the dress out.

I will wear it tonight.

Now I must go to the market."

Amelia Bedelia looked

at the bright pink dress.

"I don't see any spots.

This dress just needs washing."

Then another dress

caught Amelia Bedelia's eye.

"She must have meant
her light pink dress.
Now that one sure is spotted."
Amelia Bedelia held the dress up.
"It looks mighty nice
with the spots in it.
But I guess
she's tired of it that way."

Amelia Bedelia put spot remover on each spot.

Then she waited.

Nothing happened.

“Didn’t think
that stuff would work,”
said Amelia Bedelia.
She got the scissors.
And Amelia Bedelia
removed every spot from that dress.

"Amelia Bedelia,"
called Mrs. Rogers.
"Please take these groceries."
Amelia Bedelia ran
to take the bag.

“Here are some roses, too.
Do scatter them
around the living room.
I must get my hair done now.
While I’m gone,
wash all the vegetables
and string the beans.
If you have time,
make a jelly roll.
Great-Aunt Myra
does love jelly roll,”
said Mrs. Rogers.

Amelia Bedelia stopped

in the living room.

"Seems like roses would look nicer

sitting proper-like in vases.

But if she wants them scattered,

scattered they will be."

Amelia Bedelia went on

to the kitchen with the groceries.

She washed all the vegetables.

Then she found a ball of string.

And Amelia Bedelia

strung all those beans.

"Jelly! Roll!"
exclaimed Amelia Bedelia.
"I never heard tell
of jelly rolling."
But Amelia Bedelia
got out a jar of jelly.
Amelia Bedelia tried
again and again.
But she just could not get
that jelly to roll.

JELLY

Amelia Bedelia washed her hands.

She got out a mixing bowl.

Amelia Bedelia began to mix

a little of this

and a pinch of that.

"Great-Aunt Myra
or no Great-Aunt Myra—
there's not going to be
any rolling jelly
in this house tonight,"
said Amelia Bedelia.

Mr. and Mrs. Rogers arrived home
at the same time.
Mrs. Rogers called,
“Amelia Bedelia,
please separate three eggs
and pare the other vegetables
you washed.
I’ll do the cooking.”
Then she and Mr. Rogers
hurried upstairs to dress.

Amelia Bedelia took out three eggs.
"I wonder why they need
to be separated.
They've been together all day
and nothing happened."
But Amelia Bedelia
separated those eggs.

“Pair the vegetables!”

Amelia Bedelia laughed.

“Here, you two go together—

and you two.

Now be careful,

or I’ll be separating you, too.”

Amelia Bedelia
went up to Mrs. Rogers's room.
"What should I do
with these stripped sheets?"
she asked.
"Stripped sheets!"
exclaimed Mrs. Rogers.
But she got no further.

Mr. Rogers roared,
"What in thunderation
happened to my shirts?"
"Oh, don't you like big checks?
I didn't have time
to do little ones.
But I will next time,"
promised Amelia Bedelia.

“My dress!” exclaimed Mrs. Rogers.

“It’s full of holes.”

“Yes, ma’am, I removed

every single spot,”

said Amelia Bedelia.

Before Mrs. Rogers
could say any more,
the doorbell rang.
"Great-Aunt Myra,"
said Mr. and Mrs. Rogers.
They rushed to the front door.

"Good evening, grandniece.
Good evening, grandnephew.
My, that trip made me hungry,"
said Great-Aunt Myra.

"I'll cook dinner right now,"

said Mrs. Rogers.

Everybody went into the kitchen.

"Amelia Bedelia,
did you string the beans?"
asked Mrs. Rogers.
"Yes. See—they do
give such a homey look,"
said Amelia Bedelia.

"Where are the eggs
I asked you to separate?"
said Mrs. Rogers.
"Here's one,
one is behind the clock,
and the other is over there.
Did I separate them
far enough apart?"
asked Amelia Bedelia.
Mrs. Rogers said nothing.
So Amelia Bedelia went on.

"And I paired the vegetables.
They went together real well,
and there weren't any left over."

Mrs. Rogers slapped her hand on the table.

It hit right in a sticky blob.

"Ugh! What is that?" she shouted.

“Jelly. I tried to make it roll.

But it just plip-plopped

all over the place,”

said Amelia Bedelia.

“Amelia Bedelia!”

exclaimed Mrs. Rogers.

“How do you get things so mixed up?”

"Things mixed up!
Oh, I plumb forgot,"
said Amelia Bedelia.
She hurried to the stove.

Amelia Bedelia
opened the oven door.
Great-Aunt Myra sat up straight
and sniffed.

"Hot apple pie! I do declare.
Now that's the kind of
mixed-up thing I like."

Great-Aunt Myra announced,

"Grandniece, grandnephew,

I like it here."

"Oh, Great-Aunt Myra,

we're so glad!"

said Mr. and Mrs. Rogers.

They both began to talk at once.
But Great-Aunt Myra
wasn't much for words.
She had her eyes
on that last piece of pie.

Great-Aunt Myra put
the last piece of pie
on her plate.
Then she said,
"Grandniece, grandnephew,
I will visit you often.
That Amelia Bedelia really knows
how to make a body feel at home.
Thank you, Amelia Bedelia."

Amelia Bedelia smiled.

She and Great-Aunt Myra

would get along.

An I Can Read Book®

Amelia Bedelia and the Surprise Shower

Story by Peggy Parish

Pictures by Barbara Siebel Thomas

based on the original drawings by Fritz Siebel

For Stan,
who was born near Alcolu

There was a knock
on the back door.
"Coming, coming,"
called Amelia Bedelia.
She opened the door.

"Oh, it's you, Cousin Alcolu,"
she said. "Do come in."
"Mrs. Rogers asked me
to help out today," said Alcolu.
"Is she having a party or something?"
"Every Tuesday," said Amelia Bedelia,
"some ladies get together.
They just sew and talk.
But today Miss Alma
is in for a real surprise.
Those other ladies
are giving Miss Alma a shower!"

"A shower?" said Alcolu.

"A surprise shower!"

said Amelia Bedelia.

"Now why would they do that to her?"

asked Alcolu. "Miss Alma is nice."

"I don't know," said Amelia Bedelia.

"She is about to get married.
They should do something
nice for her.
She can give herself a shower."
"Your folks do have
funny ways," said Alcolu.

"Say, are you cooking something?"

"My cupcakes!" said Amelia Bedelia.

She ran to the oven.

"Just right," she said.

"They need to cool a bit.

Then I will ice them."

Mr. Rogers came in.

"Good morning, Amelia Bedelia.

Good morning, Alcolu,"

said Mr. Rogers.

"My, what a nice lot of fish,"

said Amelia Bedelia.

“They should taste good,” said Mr. Rogers.

“Please scale them and ice them.”

“All right,” said Amelia Bedelia.

"Say, Mr. Rogers, did you ever hear of giving somebody a surprise shower?"

"Oh, yes," said Mr. Rogers.

"It is like a surprise party.

And they shower the person with gifts.

That is why they call it a shower."

Mr. Rogers looked at his watch.

"I have to go to town," he said.

Mr. Rogers left the kitchen.

"By the way, Amelia Bedelia,"

said Alcolu, "Mrs. Rogers told me

to prune the hedge.

Could you show me how?"

"I would be glad to,"

said Amelia Bedelia.

She went to the cupboard.

She took out a box of prunes.

Amelia Bedelia and Alcolu
went to the hedge.
"Now," said Amelia Bedelia,
"you take a prune.
Then stick it on like this."
"Is that all there is to it?"
asked Alcolu.
"Prune it well," said Amelia Bedelia.
"Mrs. Rogers likes things done right."

Amelia Bedelia went into the kitchen.
"Oh, I plumb forgot
my cupcakes," she said.
"And I must make that chocolate icing."
Amelia Bedelia put some of this
and a little of that in a big pot.
She stirred and she stirred.
Then she tasted the icing.
"Just right," she said.
Amelia Bedelia began
to ice her cakes.

SUGAR
CHOCOLATE

“The fish!” she said. “Mr. Rogers said to scale them and ice them.”

Amelia Bedelia got the scales.

She piled the fish on them.

“There,” she said.

“You just scale yourselves while I ice the cakes.”

And Amelia Bedelia iced her cakes.
"Those do look nice," she said.
"And there's enough icing left
to ice the fish too."
Amelia Bedelia picked up
a fish by its tail.
"I hope you have scaled
long enough," she said.

She iced one side of the fish.

Then she iced the other side.

Amelia Bedelia worked

until the last fish was iced.

"That takes care of you," she said.

Amelia Bedelia put the iced fish
and the iced cakes in the cupboard.

Mrs. Rogers came into the kitchen.

"Amelia Bedelia, use this tablecloth

for the table," she said.

"Do run over it first with an iron.

And we need some cut flowers,"

said Mrs. Rogers.

She went out the back door.

Amelia Bedelia unfolded the tablecloth.

She put it on the floor.

Then Amelia Bedelia got the iron.

And she ran all over that tablecloth.

Amelia Bedelia put the tablecloth on the table.
Alcolu came over to Amelia Bedelia.
"That takes care of that," he said.
"I even had some prunes left.
So I pruned the other bushes too."
"That does look nice," she said.
"Mrs. Rogers will be mighty pleased."

Amelia Bedelia and Alcolu
met Mrs. Rogers at the back door.
Mrs. Rogers came in
with a bunch of flowers.
She put them on the kitchen table.

"Amelia Bedelia," she said,
"use the large silver bowl
for the cut flowers."
"All right," said Amelia Bedelia.
Mrs. Rogers left the kitchen.

She came right back
with a basket of gifts.
"These are for
Miss Alma's shower," she said.
"We will start sewing
as we always do.
Then when all the ladies are here,
we will say, Surprise!
Then comes the shower.
Can you and Alcolu
take care of everything?"
"Oh, yes," said Amelia Bedelia.
"We will see to everything."

“These flowers are so pretty,”
said Amelia Bedelia.
“It’s a shame to cut them.”
“She said cut flowers,” said Alcolu.
“Let me help you.”

So Amelia Bedelia and Alcolu

fixed a bowl of cut flowers.

"We do have some
figuring out to do," she said.
"I thought those ladies were
supposed to be giving this shower.
And here *we* are giving it."
"If we had known," said Alcolu,
"we could have fixed up
something fancy."

"It's too late for that now,"

said Amelia Bedelia.

The two of them went outside.

Amelia Bedelia saw the garden hose.

"Think that will do?" asked Alcolu.

"Well, it's not really a shower,"
said Amelia Bedelia.
"But it's the next best thing.
I will give her the gifts
and you can shower her."
"The gifts will get wet," said Alcolu.
"They are shower gifts,"
said Amelia Bedelia.
"What if they do get wet?
We will get wet too."
"Well," said Alcolu.
"We can put on something else."

“What a good idea,” said Amelia Bedelia.

“Hide those gifts first,” said Alcolu.

Amelia Bedelia hid the basket of gifts under some bushes.

“It is time to get ready,” she said.

A bit later

Amelia Bedelia heard a car stop.

"Here come the ladies,"

she called to Mrs. Rogers.

Mrs. Rogers hurried out to meet them.

Mrs. Ralph came first.

And with her came her four children.

"Look!" they shouted.

"Prunes on the hedge."

The children went racing past.

More and more ladies came.

They began to sew.

But Miss Alma did not come.

"Where is Miss Alma?" everybody asked.

But nobody knew.

Mrs. Rogers looked at the table.

"Footprints!" said Mrs. Rogers.

"Amelia Bedelia, what did you do to that tablecloth?"

"I ran over it with an iron," said Amelia Bedelia. "Should I have taken my shoes off first?"

"Oh, never mind!" said Mrs. Rogers.
"Amelia Bedelia, where are
the cut flowers?" she asked.
"Oh, my," said Amelia Bedelia.
"I forgot them."
Amelia Bedelia ran in
and got the flowers.
Mrs. Rogers looked at the bowl.
"Amelia Bedelia!" she cried.
"What did you do to those flowers?"
"I cut them," said Amelia Bedelia.
"You said to fix a bowl
of cut flowers."

Just then Miss Alma drove up.

"Here she is!" said the ladies.

"Sorry to be late," said Miss Alma.

"But I have a headache."

"I am sorry," said Mrs. Rogers.

"You just sit down."

Mrs. Rogers turned to Amelia Bedelia.

"Are you ready

for the shower?" she asked.

"We will need a minute or two,"

said Amelia Bedelia.

She called Alcolu.

They went around back.

And there stood Amelia Bedelia and Alcolu in bathing suits.

"All right," called Amelia Bedelia. "We are ready."

Then all the ladies shouted,

“SURPRISE!”

“SURPRISE!” shouted Amelia Bedelia.
She ran out with the gifts
and dumped them on Miss Alma’s lap.
“Here are the gifts,” she said.

Alcolu came right behind her

with the hose.

"And here is the shower!" he shouted.

“A shower! A shower!”
screamed Mrs. Ralph’s four children.
And they jumped into the shower
with Miss Alma.

All the ladies screamed too.

And they jumped out of the shower.

Miss Alma leaped up.

Her gifts flew all over the place.

"How dare you!" she shouted.

Miss Alma was angry.

She was very angry.

“Amelia Bedelia! Alcolu!”

shouted Mrs. Rogers.

“Turn off that water this minute.”

Amelia Bedelia and Alcolu

turned off the water.

"Did you see how mad
Miss Alma was?" asked Alcolu.
"I don't think she liked our shower,"
said Amelia Bedelia.
"Maybe some hot tea will help her."
Amelia Bedelia and Alcolu
went into the kitchen.
"I'll take the tea things,"
said Amelia Bedelia.
"You bring the cupcakes.
Here is the tea," said Amelia Bedelia.
"Thank goodness for that,"
said Mrs. Rogers.

"Hmmm, that chocolate looks good,"
said Mrs. Ralph.

"Help yourself," said Mrs. Rogers.

Mrs. Ralph helped herself

to the biggest piece.

She took her fork.

Mrs. Ralph tried to cut it.

But it would not cut.

And Mrs. Ralph wanted that chocolate.

So she picked it up and bit it.

"Uuggg," she screamed.

"Fish! Raw fish!"

Mrs. Ralph was angry.

She was very angry.

Mr. Rogers came out just then.

He heard what Mrs. Ralph said.

"Fish!" he shouted. "Amelia Bedelia!

What did you do to my fish?"

"Iced them!" said Amelia Bedelia.

Now Mr. Rogers was angry too.

Suddenly Miss Alma started laughing.
Everybody looked at her.
She jumped up and threw her arms
around Amelia Bedelia.
"You are wonderful!"
said Miss Alma.
"My headache is all gone.
That surprise shower
was just what I needed."

Then Mrs. Ralph laughed.
"Amelia Bedelia," she asked,
"did you prune the hedge?"
"Cousin Alcolu did that,"
said Amelia Bedelia.
"Then he is wonderful too,"
said Mrs. Ralph.

"See how happy my children are.
They have never been this good."

And suddenly everybody was laughing.

Mrs. Rogers began
to pour the tea.
Amelia Bedelia served
the chocolate cupcakes.
And the ladies said they were
the best cakes they had ever eaten.
"That was so much fun,"
said all the ladies,
and they laughed some more.
Then they helped pick up
Miss Alma's gifts.

And they were still laughing when they left.